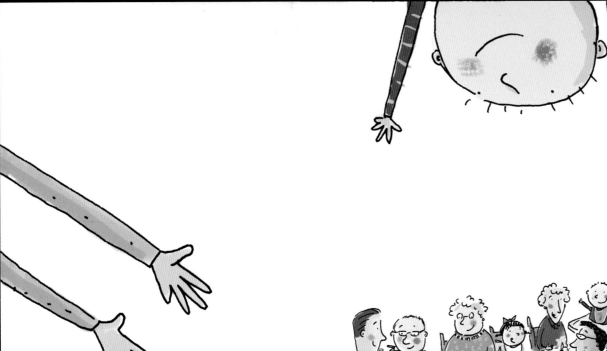

Text copyright © 2005 by Harriet Ziefert
Pictures copyright © 2005 by Deborah Zemke
All rights reserved
CIP Data is available.
Published in the United States 2005 by
Blue Apple Books
515 Valley Street, Maplewood, N.J. 07040
www.blueapplebooks.com
Distributed in the U.S. by Chronicle Books
First Edition
Printed in China
ISBN: 1-59354-071-X

1 3 5 7 9 10 8 6 4 2

Families Have Together

Harriet Ziefert

pictures by Deborah Zemke

🍎 Blue Apple Books

For Jon's family
and Jamie's family—
each with their
own style

—H.M.Z.

For my near
and dear

—D.Z.

Morning has hugs.

Toasters have plugs.

Breakfast has mugs.

Milk has glugs.

Pots
have
cooks.

Moms have
"eat-your-breakfast"
looks.

Spoons have beat.

Hands have eat.

Hair has brush.

School days have . . .

RUSH!

Jackets have zips.

Shoelaces have trips.

Chairs have tips.

Kids have sobs.

Mommies
have
jobs.

(So do daddies.)

(So do children.)

Clocks have tick.

Kittens have lick.

Fingers have click.

Feet have kick.

Brussels sprouts
have
ICK!

Leaves have rakes.

Birthdays have cakes.

Bellies have aches.

Wagons have tow.

Noses have blow.

Feet have grow.

Bottoms have sit.
Hats have fit.

Hands have hold.

Winter has cold.

Arms have **wide**.

Skis have slide.

Grandpas
have
sneezes.

Grandmas
have
squeezes.

Thank-yous have pleases.

Father has Mother.

Sister has Brother.

We all have each other.

Raisins have wrinkles.

Cookies have sprinkles.

Stars have twinkles.

Holidays have dinners.

Games have winners.

Backpacks have zips.

Bikes
have
grips.

Soda has sips.

Families have trips.

Stories have tell.

Mommies have YELL!

(So do daddies.)

Kids have "but!"

Doors have shut.

Haircuts have snips.

Puppies have yips.

Skirts have hide.

Cars have ride.

Families have friends.

Roads have bends.

Vacations have camping.

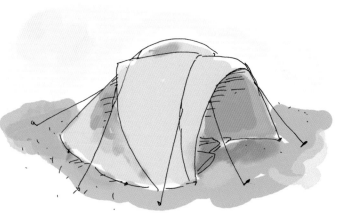

Hikes have tramping

Bathrooms have doors.

Sleepers have snores.

Rain has pours!

Summer has weather.

Families have . . .

together!